Handbook

Harmonium

HISTORY | *ANATOMY* | *TUNING* | *MAINTENANCE*

Handbook of
Harmonium

HISTORY | ANATOMY | TUNING | MAINTENANCE

By

Pankaj Vishal

PANKAJ PUBLICATIONS
New Delhi, INDIA

Handbook of Harmonium
First Published May, 2008
Copyright © Pankaj Publications

ISBN 13: 978-81-87155-98-0
ISBN 10: 81-87155-98-1

Published by :
PANKAJ PUBLICATIONS
M-114, Vikas Puri
New Delhi 110 018
Email : contact@pankajmusic.com
ⓦ www.pankajmusic.com

For bulk purchases and business inquiries,
contact@ pankajmusic.com

Cover design by	:	Square Vision
Typesetting by	:	Reliable Infomedia
Illustrations	:	Reliable Infomedia & Mohit Suneja
Printed in India by	:	

All rights reserved.
This work is the author's own tested work, and he has
right to recognise any violations made to this copy.
No part of this book may be reproduced, stored in a re-
trieval system or transmitted in any form or by any means
electronic, mechanical, photocopying recording or otherwise, without prior written permission of the publisher.

Preface

꽃 ════════════════════════════════════ ಚಿ

Movement and Harmony is the primary quality of nature. Look at the Sun, the Moon, the Stars, the Planets ... the Milky Way, even the entire universe, everything is in continuous motion and in perfect harmony. The strange thing about the motion of these things is that they are in perfect rhythm. Similarly, music also gets its identity due to its quality of rhythm and harmony with the notes.

Instrumental Music is one of the major forms of music which constitute a separate branch altogether. Therefore, it is important in life.

Keeping this in mind, we would like to introduce to the readers one of the most important instruments of Indian Music Tradition - the Harmonium. The Harmonium is a popular musical instrument in the world and it has a respectable place in Indian Music also. This book gives you a sound idea of the history, development and basics of the instrument, to begin with and motivates the reader by enhancing his interest to know more about this wonderful instrument to proceed further.

This book takes proper care of the inquisitiveness of the beginners and point out the salient probable problem areas of this field in a friendly manner.

Any suggestion for improvement of this book is welcome.

PANKAJ VISHAL

Publishers' Note

The PANKAJ PUBLICATIONS is an undisputed leader and pioneer in the field of music books. The house is in continuous service to music lovers spread all over the world by promoting Indian music religiously by the way of its books, C.D.s, journals and assisting practicing musicians.

A series of books with vital information about the musical instruments, its origin, evolution, playing technique, etc. was in great demand for the last couple of years. In view of the larger interest of the readers and music lovers, we have brought this series of 'Handbooks' at lowest possible price to meet the needs of readers.

The entire editorial team of the PANKAJ PUBLICATIONS carried out intensive research and came out with the fruits in the form of these books. We hope this series will be of immense help to people as our previous series of 'Pankaj Learn to play' proved to be.

If we are successful in our mission, although in a little amount, the entire team along with this publication will be proud of the effort.

- *PUBLISHER*

Contents

Part – 1
Theory of Music

The Indian Music System

Indian Music is based on *Ragas* and *Ragas* are based on *the Nadas, Shrutis, Swaras, Saptaka* and *Thaats*, as shown in the evolution chart.

Nada (Sound) : This is sound produced by striking, friction or beating. *'Nada'* is of two kinds:

(a) *Sangeet-un-upyogi Nada* **(Non-Musical sound)**: Those sounds which are not musical such as machine rattlings, traffic horns, shouting etc. These sounds are not pleasant to listen to and are disturbing in nature. They can cause headaches and irritation. We hear these sounds in our day-to-day lives in the city.

(b) *Sangeet-upyogi Nada* **(Musical sound):** Contrary to non-musical sounds, these sounds are pleasant to listen to and musically audible. These can be the sounds of nature as the chirping of birds, water falls, flowing river, singing etc. These sounds are relaxing and give a feeling of tranquility and peace. Musical sounds like singing and instrumental playing have the virtue to hypnotize an audience.

Shruti **(Microtonal Interval notes)**: These are microtonal sounds found between **Sangeet-upyogi Nadas** (musical sounds). They can be heard and distinguished by a sensitive musical ear only. They can now be seen visually on an 'Oscilloscope'. *Shrutis* are also called Microtonal Intervals of Sound. The gaps are increased between the sounds to make these **Shrutis** to **notes** for the purpose of easy recognition and the development of music by using them when playing and singing.

11

There are 22 *Shrutis* used in Indian Music.

1. Tivra	8. Raudri	15. Rakta
2. Kumudwati	9. Krodhi	16. Sandipini
3. Manda	10. Vajrika	17. Alapini
4. Chhandovati	11. Prasarini	18. Madanti
5. Dayawati	12. Priti	19. Rohini
6. Ranjani	13. Manjari	20. Romya
7. Raktika	14. Kshiti	21. Ugra
		22. Kshobhini

Swaras (Notes): *Swaras* (notes) are produced by *Shrutis* with big intervals or Gaps. They can be distinguished by the ears of listeners. The difference between 'Swaras' and 'Shrutis' is that the 'Swaras' are measured by *Shrutis* depending on the intervals or number of *Shrutis*.

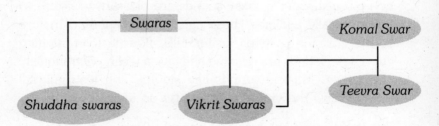

Swaras are of two types, *Vikrits* **Swara (Distorted note)** and **Shuddha Swara (Full Tone note)**

Shuddha Swaras (Full Tone Notes). These are natural notes which are found in the *Shrutis*. To recognize the minute gap of *Shrutis* easily.

Shudha Swaras or Full Tone Notes were identified and called **Natural notes** and they are 7 of them.

Vedic names along with the popular short names of these 7 notes are given below. The complete music theory is based on these 7 notes and their combinations.

S. No.	Name of Swaras	Shuddha Swaras	Western Notes	Shruti
1.	Shadaj	Sa	C	4 Tivra, Kumudwati, Manda Chhandovati.
2.	Rishabh	Re	D	3 Dayawati, Ranjani, Raktika
3.	Gandhar	Ga	E	2 Raudri & Krodhi
4.	Madhyam	Ma	F	4 Vajrika, Prasarini, Priti, Manjari
5.	Pancham	Pa	G	4 Kshiti, Rakta, Sandipini Alapini
6.	Dhaiwat	Dha	A	3 Madanti, Rohini, Romya
7.	Nishad	Ni	B	2 Ugra Kshobhini

With the identification of these full tone notes the gap between the notes becomes wider. The wider the gap the greater the obstruction to the sweetness of sound. Musicians then introduced **Half Tone Notes** or **Flat Notes** (Komal Swaras) between two **Full Tone Notes** (Shuddha Swaras), and thus **Distorted notes** (Vikrit Swaras) came into existance.

Vikrit Swaras **(Distorted Notes)** : *Vikrit Swar*as are of two types, they are *Komal Swar*as (Flat Notes or Half Tone Notes) and *Tivra Swara* (Sharp note). With the introduction of the distorted notes, *Sa* and *Pa* though remained unchanged.

Komal Swaras **(Flat notes or Half Tone Notes)** are found between two **shudha swaras (Full Tone notes)**. These *Swar*as are a bit lower in pitch from the *Shuddha Swar*as. They are symbolized in notation by a Dash (_) below the note such as **Re**. A half step lower.

※ There are four *Komal Swar*as (flat notes). These are: **Re, Ga, Dha, & Ni.**

Tivra Swar is the note which appears a half step above the full note and is called a **sharp note (*Tivra Swar*)**. This *Swar* (note) is higher in pitch from the *Shuddha Swara*. It is symbolized in notation by a small vertical line (⎮) over the note.

※ There is only one *Tivra Swar,* which is **Ma**.

According to two different notation systems, it is important to understand the difference between the two. There are two fixed notes in Indian system. These are **Sa & Pa**. The remaining five notes have two different types as semitone or distorted forms. On the other hand there are two types for all the seven notes in the western system. There is a distortion of each note and all the notes can be either flat or sharp. The closest related western note to the Indian distorted notes are as follows -

Indian Notes	Re	Ga	Ma	Dha	Ni
Western Notes	C# or D♭	D# or E♭	F# or G♭	G# or A♭	A# or B♭

1. As shown in the table, note **komal Re** is shown as it is but in western system, it is written as two types, either **C#** or **D♭**. Where (**#**) symbol is used for sharp (*tivra*) and (♭) symbol is used for flat (*komal*).

2. There are two fixed notes in the Indian system. These are **Sa** & **Pa**, which cannot be changed to flats or sharp.

3. Western music does not have sharp for note **E** & **B**. Instead, **F** stands for **E#**, and **C** stands for **B#**.

This is how the Twelve notes come to exist. They are as follows.

Sl. No.	Swaras	Description	Western Name
1.	Sa	*Shudha* (Fixed)	**C Fixed**
2.	Re	*Komal*	D Half Tone note
3.	**Re**	***Shuddha***	**D Full tone note**
4.	Ga	*Komal*	E Half tone note
5.	**Ga**	***Shuddha***	**E Full tone note**
6.	**Ma**	***Shudha***	**F Full tone note**
7.	Ma	*Tivra*	F Sharp note
8.	**Pa**	***Shuddha*** (Fixed)	**G Fixed**
9.	Dha	*Komal*	A Half tone note
10.	**Dha**	***Shuddha***	**A Full note**
11.	Ni	*Komal*	B Half Tone note
12.	**Ni**	***Shuddha***	**B Full Note**

A group of these 7 Natural Notes (*Shuddha Swaras*) make a *Saptak* (Octave). The *Saptak* also includes 4 *Komal* and one *Tivra Swar*. In all there are 12 Notes to make a complete **Saptak (Octave).** A *Saptak* (Octave) includes the *guru* notes of Indian Music which are **Sa Re Ga Ma Pa Dha Ni.** A specific combination of these *Swar*as (Notes) from the *Saptak* forms a **Thaat (scale),** which is the basis of the *Ragas*.

Ragas (Melodies) are a particular combination of these notes or group of notes, which are produced from **Thaats (scales)**.

In a nutshell, we can understand the journey of swaras from its origin to Nada by this evolution chart.

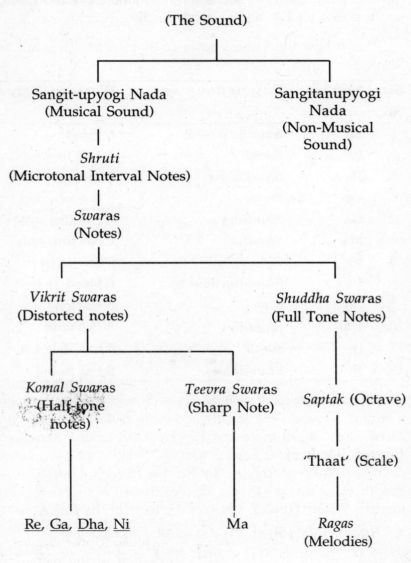

NADA
(The Sound)

Sangit-upyogi Nada
(Musical Sound)

Sangitanupyogi Nada
(Non-Musical Sound)

Shruti
(Microtonal Interval Notes)

*Swar*as
(Notes)

*Vikrit Swar*as
(Distorted notes)

*Shuddha Swar*as
(Full Tone Notes)

*Komal Swar*as
(Half-tone notes)

*Teevra Swar*as
(Sharp Note)

Saptak (Octave)

'Thaat' (Scale)

Re, Ga, Dha, Ni

Ma

Ragas
(Melodies)

SAPTAK (Octave)

According to the Indian theory of music there are three ranges of the human voice, which are low, medium and high pitch. These pitches when identified with notes in music called *Saptaka* or a group of seven *Shuddha* notes. These seven notes also includes four *komal* and one *Tivra Swara*. The human voice is differentiated under these three ranges:

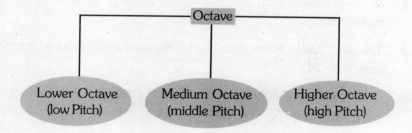

1. **Madhya Saptaka** (Medium Octave) — When the sound naturally comes out of the throat without any pressure, it is called the throat voice. The Medium octave or *Madhya Saptaka*.

2. **Mandra Saptaka** (Lower Octave) — When the sound comes out entirely by the pressure of the lungs, it is called the chest voice or *Mandra Saptaka* (Lower Octave). In this *Saptaka* the pitch of the sound is lower than the medium octave.

3. **Tar Saptaka** (Upper Octave) — When the sound is produced with the exertion of force on the nostrils and head, called the head voice or *Tar Saptaka* (Upper Octave). The pitch or sound is higher than that of the medium octave.

THAAT

Ordinarily a *Thaat* is a combination of **seven Swaras** or notes capable of producing *Ragas*. All the notes played in *thaat* are in ascending order starting from **Sa** ending at **Ni,** whether natural, flat or sharp. There are basically ten *thaats* in Indian music system.

The *Thaat* must qualify these three Basic conditions :

1. A *Thaat* must contain the seven *swaras* (notes) in the regular form.

2. The *Shuddha*, *Komal* or *Tivra Swaras* must appear one after the other.

3. It is a mere scale, a combination of notes. It does not essentially need to please the listeners ear.

Ten thaats and their notes as follows:

1. Bilawal	Sa	Re	Ga	Ma	Pa	Dha	Ni
2. Khamaj	Sa	Re	Ga	Ma	Pa	Dha	<u>Ni</u>
3. Kafee	Sa	Re	<u>Ga</u>	Ma	Pa	Dha	<u>Ni</u>
4. Asawari	Sa	Re	<u>Ga</u>	Ma	Pa	<u>Dha</u>	<u>Ni</u>
5. Bhairav	Sa	<u>Re</u>	Ga	Ma	Pa	<u>Dha</u>	Ni
6. Kalyan	Sa	Re	Ga	Ma'	Pa	Dha	Ni
7. Poorvi	Sa	<u>Re</u>	Ga	Ma	Pa	<u>Dha</u>	Ni
8. Bhairavi	Sa	<u>Re</u>	<u>Ga</u>	Ma	Pa	<u>Dha</u>	<u>Ni</u>
9. Todi	Sa	<u>Re</u>	<u>Ga</u>	Ma'	Pa	<u>Dha</u>	Ni
10. Marva	Sa	<u>Re</u>	Ga	Ma	Pa	Dha	Ni

RAGAS

A *Raga* is a combination of sounds or *swaras* having qualities that give pleasure to the listener. Every *Raga* has a peculiar quality of its own. To be acquainted with *Ragas,* a musician should bear in mind the following points :

1. *Ragas* must belong to a *Thaat.*

2. At least five notes are essential for a *Raga.*

3. In a *Raga* the melody is very essential.

4. A *Raga* must have its own ascent, descent (*Aroha* and *avaroha*) and fixed notes *(Vadi & Samvadi).*

5. The **Sa** *Swara* (C note) is the same note (fixed) in every *Raga*, and both **Ma** & **Pa** are not to be omitted at the same time.

Parts of combination of a raga

There are 4 distinguished parts of a raga/composition/song.

1. Sthayi : First part (face) or introduction.

2. Antara : Second part or body.

3. Sanchari : Combinarion of notes of 'Sthayi' & 'Antara'.

4. Abhog : Some notes of the composition played in the upper octave.

Categories of Ragas (*Jati' of a Raga*)

The following are the three most common categories of Ragas :

1. **Sampurna** has seven notes ascending and descending.

2. **Shadava** has six notes ascending and descending.

3. **Odava** has five notes in the same *Swaras*, both ascending & descending.

Categories of Ragas

S. No.	Category	No. of Swaras		Total No. of Ragas with the Combination of Ascending & Descending Notes
		Ascent	Descent	
1.	Sampurna–Sampurna	7	7	1 – 1 x 1 – 1
2.	Shadava–Shadava	6	6	6 – 6 x 6 – 36
3.	Odava–Odava	5	5	15 – 15x15– 225
4.	Sampurna–Shadava	7	6	6 – 1 x 6 – 6
5.	Sampurna–Odava	7	5	15 – 1 x 15 – 15
6.	Shadva–Sampurna	6	7	6 – 6 x 1 – 6
7.	Shadva–Odava	6	5	90 – 6 x 15 – 90
8.	Odava–Sampurna	5	7	15 – 15 x 1 – 15
9.	Odava–Shadava	5	6	90 – 15 x 6 – 90

Lay (Tempo or Speed)

LAY : (Tempo)

In the ordinary sense **lay** means Beat or speed or any regular space of time between boundaries to complete a circle in a specific time period. It is a natural harmonious flow of vocal and instrumental sound with a regular succession of accents. There is no fixed structure of speed or tempo in music. Every musician chooses it according to his convenience; but basically, what is important is that one should be able to control the *lay* or tempo of *taal*. The tempo should neither be too slow nor should it be extraordinarily fast. Not only this, even in a slow tempo it should be in such a manner that it can entertain the audience on the one hand and on the other its musicality will not be sacrificed.

Normally a slow tempo should be half the tempo of a standard one and a fast tempo should be double that of the standard. But again it differs according to the capabilitiy of the musician. An expert musician starts the tempo in a very slow pace and gradually increases it reaching the required speed.

According to observations there are mainly three types of beat which have been accepted in the Indian music. But there is one more special type called '*Ati Drut Lay*', which is generally used by expert musicians, because tempo in this particular type is very fast and very tough to control. All percussion instruments are used to control and regularize the musical sound.

21

The Three types of beats are :

1. **Madhya Lay** (Medium or Normal Beat).
   eg. 1 2 3 4

2. **Drut Lay** (Quick or Fast Beat).
   eg. 1 2 3 4

3. **Vilambit Lay** (Slow Beat).
   eg. 1   2   3   4

(Note the space between the numbers)

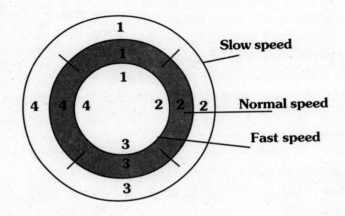

Normal Tempo

Normal Beat is the time required by a musician to complete a round or a part of a song, tune or dance in a comfortable speed without any stress. Although no fix structure is available for this, convenience is the key. The tempo should be easy enough within the musician's control. In a normal speed any composition whether instrumental or vocal leaves a very refreshing effect on the audience. The Normal beat is the basis of the remaining two beats.

Eg. 1 2 3 4 1 2 3 4 etc.

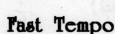

Fast Tempo

Fast Beat means half the time of a normal beat. This is when a musician, say, requires one minute of time to complete a part of a song, tune or dance, in normal beat, now he will require half the time taken by the normal beat. In other words we can say that the musician can take two rounds of his play for the time required in the normal beat.

Eg. 1 2 3 4-1 2 3 4-1 2 3 4 etc.

Slow Tempo

In Slow Beat a musician takes double the time to complete the round required by the medium or normal beat. Suppose if he completes a round of his song in one minute in normal beat, he will now take two minutes to complete the same song.

Eg. 1 - 2 - 3 - 4 - 1 - 2 - 3 - 4   etc.

Comparative speeds in various beats:

Slow beat	: 1		2		3		4	
Medium Beat	: 1	2	3	4	1	2	3	4
Fast Beat	: 1 2 3 4	1 2 3 4	1 2 3 4	1 2 3 4

Taal (The Rhythm)

Taal or Rhythm is the regular succession of sound vibrations, necessary to make sound musical. It is a scale for producing the rhythmic pattern in a song or *Raga*. Each song or composition runs on a particular time scale, and the scale is repeated in a particular gap, this gap is repeated for a specific number of times, which makes the rhythm cycle for the composition. The gaps between the notes in a scale is known as intervals, which can be created by clapping, or by a percussion instrument. The most popular is the Tabla. The early Indian musicians invented many *taals* of different *matras* (Rhythms), *Khand* (Bars) and *Bols* (Sounds) and fixed the points of *'Sam'*, *Talis* and *Khalis* for every *Taal*.

Beat : As we know well now, beat is a time-scale map in a composition. The common beats in the Indian system are *Kehrava Taal* (8 beats) and *Daadara taal* (6 beats).

Beat and its part in a composition is written and understood by some technical names like *sam, tali, khali,* etc. in the Indian music system. These terms and names carry a lot of importance for the beginners to understand. Let's learn them in detail.

Bol (Sounds) : Each beat is made out of notes or sounds. These sounds can be of percussions or of melody notes. The sounds created by percussions like drums or tabla, played as accompaniment or are spoken as **Dha, Dhin,** etc. are known as Bols.

Sam : The starting point of a taal notation or a beat cycle, from the point where the beat starts in a composition is known as **Sam.** This is the point in a notation where all the instruments stops and start together when playing many instruments together. It is shown in the notation with **(x)** sign.

Taali : Literally means the clap, it is the particular point in a notation where maximum pressure is given to the playing. This is also the repeated starting point of a part in a beat cycle.

24

For example; as shown below, while playing "*Teen Taal*" 1st, 5th, & 13th bol has *taali* in its place -

Beat signs	×				2			
Beat	1	2	3	4	5	6	7	8
Bol	Dha	Dhin	Dhin	Dha	Dha	Dhin	Dhin	Dha
Beat signs	0				3			
Beat	9	10	11	12	13	14	15	16
Bol	Dha	Tin	Tin	Ta	Ta	Dhin	Dhin	Dha

Khali : Khali literally means empty space, which is actually not, only the force or emphasis of sound is less in this part. *Khali* in a composition means a gap of some *matras* within *boles* of *Theka* played by the right hand on the Tabla only while the left (*Duggi* or *Dhama*) remains silent in *khali matra* time. This is a point in a notation where comparatively less force is given to the *bol*. For example, while playing "*teen taal*", the 9th beat in the cycle is the space for *khali*.

Parts: Putting all the sounds in a group separated by *sam, tali* and *khali* are known as parts or measures. Parts are shown in notation by a vertical line between the group of notes or sounds. For example: *Daadra taal* is of two parts with 3 sounds per measure:

Beat signs	×			0		
Beat	1	2	3	4	5	6
Bol	Dha	Dhin	Na	Ta	Tin	Na

All the symbols such as *sam, tali, khali* are placed on the 1st note of the group.

Sthayi : First part or the introduction of the song or a composition which is repeated in the song after paragraphs is called *sthayi*.

Antara : The second part or the middle part of the song which is also known as the body is called *Antara*.

Some Important Beats

Keherva Taal

It is the most popular and common *Taal* used in Indian Light Music. It has 8 '*matras*' or beat with **sam** on the 1st beat and **khali** on the 5th. *Ghazal* and *Bhajan* & Light music get beautiful expression in this *taal*. This *taal* is relatively easy to learn and understand and therefore very popular among musicians.

Parts/Measures - 2   *Beats - 8*
one taali & one Khali

Beat signs	x				0			
Beat	1	2	3	4	5	6	7	8
Bol		Dha	Ge	Na	Ti	Na	Ka	Dhi	Na

Dadra Taal

This is another popular *taal* of Indian Light Music. It consists of 6 *matras* with *sam* on the 1st and *khali* on 5th. Any composition of '*Sringar Ras*' will suit this *taal*. Generally *Thumri*, *Bhajans* and *Ghazals* are sung in this *taal*. This *taal* is very easy to grasp and learn, therefore it is very much in use in the field of music.

Parts/Measures - 2   *Beats - 6*
one taali & one Khali

Beat signs	×			0		
Beat	1	2	3	4	5	6
Bol	Dha	Dhin	Na	Dha	Tin	Na

Roopak Taal

One of the most popular *taals* of Indian Music; used both in light as well as classical music. It has 7 beats with *sam* on the 1st and *taali* on 5th & 7th *matras*. Some musicians believe that *khali* is on the 1st. Classical compositions as well as light *bhajans* and *ghazals* are made to flourish in this *taal* very extensively. Being a *taal* of odd numbers it is very impulsive and its least numbers of beat make it easier to grasp and control.

Parts/Measures - 3
Two taali & one Khali

Beats - 7

Beat signs	×			2		3	
Beat	1	2	3	4	5	6	7
Bol	Tin	Tin	Na	Dhin	Na	Dhin	Na

(**Note :** Roopak taal starts from sam, so the taali is not given there.)

Deep Chandi Taal

This *taal* is usually used in classical music only. It has 14 beats with *sam* on the 1st. This *taal* is generally used by expert musicians. Although light composition can be sung or played in this *taal* but it is not so easy to handle. Medium tempo compositions are used in this *taal*.

Parts/Measures - 4
Three taali & one Khali

Beats - 14

Beat signs	×			2			
Beat	1	2	3	4	5	6	7
Bol	Dha	Dhin	S	Dha	Dha	Tin	S
Beat signs	0			3			
Beat	8	9	10	11	12	13	14
Bol	Ta	Tin	S	Dha	Dha	Dhin	S

Teen Taal

This is the base of all *taals* in Indian Music. It has 16 beats with *sam* on 1st, 2nd taali on 5th, *khali* on 9th and 3rd *taali* on 13th. It is called base of all taals because *every* other *taal* is in the fraction of *teen taal*. It is easy to learn and most widely used in music both light and classical. Slow and medium and fast compositions are played and sung in this *taal*.

Parts/Measures - 4   *Beats - 16*
Three taali & one Khali

Beat signs	×				2			
Beat	1	2	3	4	5	6	7	8
Bol	Dha	Dhin	Dhin	Dha	Dha	Dhin	Dhin	Dha
Beat signs	0				3			
Beat	9	10	11	12	13	14	15	16
Bol	Dha	Tin	Tin	Ta	Ta	Dhin	Dhin	Dha

Jhap Taal

This *taal* too is very popular but mostly used in classical music. it has 10 matras with *sam* on 1st and 2nd *taali* on 5th, *khali* on 9th and 3rd taali on 10th. Composition in slow and medium tempo is generally used in this *taal*. Although light compositions can be made in this *taal* but generally it is not because its rhythm pattern is somewhat different and not so easy to learn and grasp compared to other *taals*.

Parts/Measures - 4   *Beats - 10*
Three taali & one Khali

Beat signs	×		2		0			3		
Beat	1	2	3	4	5	6	7	8	9	10
Bol	Dhin	Na	Dhin	Dhin	Na	Tin	Na	Dhin	Dhin	Na

Ek Taal

One of the popular *taals* of Indian music system. This *taal* is used in classical music but may be used in light music also. It has 12 *matras* with *sam* on the 1st beat. Slow and fast tempo compositions are used in this *taal*. This *taal* has three times the beat that of *Dadra taal* and hence its rhythm pattern is similar to the later. This *taal* is easy to learn and grasp and is impulsive in nature.

Parts/Measures - 6   *Beats - 12*
Four taali & Two Khali

Beat signs	×		0		2	
Beat	1	2	3	4	5	6
Bol	Dhin	Dhin	DhaGe	TirKit	Tu	Na
Beat signs	0		3		4	
Beat	7	8	9	10	11	12
Bol	Kat	Ta	DhaGe	TirKit	Dhin	Na

Teevra Taal

It is also a popular and old *taal* of Indian music system. Initially it was played on pakhawaj only but now it is widely played in tabla also. Similar to *Roopak* this *taal* has 7 beats. This *taal* is used in classical music only in medium or slow tempo. Its nature is very intense and therefore is used in serious music such as *Dhrupad* and *khayal* etc.

Parts/Measures - 3   *Beats - 7*
Three taali

Beat signs	×			2		3	
Beat	1	2	3	4	5	6	7
Bol	Dha	Din	Ta	Tit	Kat	GaDe	Gin

Indian Music Notation System

Tips to Read a Composition

1. **Shudha Swaras (Full tone Notes):** No sign is required i.e. Sa. Re, Ga, Ma, Pa, Dha, Ni. Only the first letter is required in the notation i.e. S, R, G, M, P, D, N.

2. **Komal Swaras (Half Tone Notes):** A dash (—) is written under the notes i.e. R̲ G̲ D̲ N̲.

3. **Tivra Swara (Sharp Note):** A small perpendicular line is placed over the note i.e. Ḿ.

4. **Madhya Saptak Swaras (Medium Octave Notes):** No sign is required for this octave notes i.e. S R G M P D N.

5. **Mandra Saptak Swaras (Lower Octave Notes):** A dot is written under the notes i.e. Ṣ Ṛ G Ṃ Ṗ Ḍ Ṇ

6. **Ati Mandra Saptak Swaras (Double lower octave):** Two dots are written under the notes i.e. **S̤ P̤**

7. **Tar Saptak Swaras (Upper Octave Notes):** A dot is written over the notes S R G M P D N

8. **Matras** are shown in numbers 1 2 3 4 5 6 etc. Normally one note shows one *Matra* time.

9. **Tali:** Numbers written between the bars.

10. **Khali:** A Zero (0) is shown in a bar.

11. **Sam:** A sign of (×) is written on the first matra of every *Taal*.

30

12. **Khand (Bar):** Vertical lines drawn indicating divisions of *Taals.*

13. **Extending or prolonging** of Notes, a dash (—) is written after the notes. One dash shows one matra time.

	1st Khand		2nd Khand	3rd Khand
Sam	Tali	Khali	Tali
×	2	0	3
Matras 1 2 3 4	5 6 7 8	9 10 11 12	13 14 15 16

14. Two, Three or Four notes in a ***matra*** time. These notes are combined together by a bracket under the notes i.e.SR SRG SRGM

15. **Jhala (Vamping):** To express *Jhala* normally "*J*" sign is used. But traditionally and mostly a space is mentioned (–) as *jhala* with notes.

16. **Meend:** Meend is shown by a semicircular line over the notes i.e. SG SM SP.

17. **Chikari:** Small (c) is written after the note. i.e. Sc, Rc,Gc.

18. **Kan Swara (Grace note):** Small letter is written in superscript by the side of the main note on the right.

M^G P^M

19. **Prolonging, Pause or Extending the note length:** Dashes are placed after a note, one dash is fixed for one matra time.

i.e. S—, R— —,G— —.

Format of Music on Harmonium

We have learned a lot about the theory of music and at the same time are familiar with the fundamentals of the music. In another words we now know how to play natural and flat or sharp notes on sitar. But there is a great confusion when we start playing. After playing the basic notes our mind wonders what next ? What should be played thereafter when we have played so called basics of music. Every instrument has its own unique features and hence every instrument has some fixed protocol according to which they are played. Our Harmonium is no exception to this rule. Here in Harmonium there are certain ways which are fixed and the Harmonium is played according to that rule only. When we talk about this rule, we find out how music in produced on Harmonium which is soothing and appealing to the audience.

Basically Harmonium is a instrument on which every type of music is played. When we are playing light music on it we play the tune of the song only, But when we play classical music on Harmonium, its playing technique is slightly different. So, lets understand how music is played on the Harmonium when we are playing it as solo instrument.

We start from "Aalap", which is a introduction to "Raga". Aalap is spread in three octaves. Here the artist shows his imagination and different permutation and combination of notes which are used in the Raga. After finishing it we start "Jod". Jod is a technique in which actual rhythm is not played but it is very much in rhythm. Different tempos are used to play the Jod. First of all we start with slow tempo and gradually we increase out speed and play different "Taans" also. At a critical

32

rate of speed the tempo of Jod so fast that it takes the form of "*Jhala*". Again this is the Jhala in which no rhythm is played but the Jhala itself is in rhythm. After finishing *Jhala* the Tabla comes in and we play "*Vilambit* Gat". Here the artist shows his mastery over the *Raga* and pours the notes in different melodious combination. Thereafter "*Drut* Gat" is played. In Drut Gat the artist shows his command over the speed and tempo. Gradually increasing the speed the artist finishes with Jhala.

When we are playing Harmonium as an accompanist we follow only what the main artist is singing. In accompanying, we does not require anything to do from our own and merely dependent on the main performing artist.

Western Notation System

The Western notation system is based on time symbols and where they are placed on the staff. These signs show both the *Swaras* and the length of time. These symbols are the notes, written on a set of 5 horizontal lines and 4 equal spaces between them called the Staff. There are two sets of the staff on which music notes are written: one for the lower tones or sounds and the other for the higher tones or sounds. The **lower tones or pitches** are represented by the **Bass** (*pronounced base*) **Staff** on which the Bass Clef Sign (𝄢) is written and the **higher tones or pitches** and **medium tones or pitches** are represented by the **Treble Staff** on which the Treble clef sign (𝄞) is written. Together these two staves make the **Grand Staff.**

The symbols of notes used in western music and their near meanings in Indian Music are given below.

Symbols of Notes		Sound Values
Whole Note or Semi-breve	o	4 beats)*Matra*) of sound
Half Note or Minim	♩	2 beats (*Matra*) of sound
Quarter Note or Crotchet	♩	1 beat (*Matra*) of sound
Dotted Half Note or Dotted Minim	♩.	3 beats (*Matra*) of sound
Eighth Note or Quaver	♪	½ beat (*Matra*) of sound
16th Note or Semi-quaver	♬	¼ (*Matra*) beat of sound

Symbols of Notes		Sound Values
Full Tone Notes or Naturals	♮	Shudh Swaras (denoted as SRGMPDN)
Half Tone Notes or Flats	♭	Komal Swaras (denotes with line under the note: S <u>RG</u> MP <u>DM</u>)
Sharp Note	♯	Tivra Swara (denote with a vertcal line over the note; SRGṀPDN
Bass Cleff sign	𝄢	Mandra Saptaka (denote with a '•' under the note; S R G M P D N
Treble Cleff sign	𝄞	Tar saptak (denote with a '•' over the notes: S R G M P D N

Apart from the above symbols in western music the beat is also very important. In fact it is the backbone of all music. Without the beat there is no music. The beat in music is related to Time which is Space between measuring units which are numbers. Without numbers we cannot measure time or any form of measurement for that matter. Hence Time maybe defined as space between numbers. So also the beat in music which is *Equal spaces of time between numbers*. These spaces must be equal in music otherwise it is just noise. This means if we have a piece of music that has four beats

the 1st beat will be the **space** between numbers 1 and 2

the 2nd beat will be the **space** between numbers 2 and 3

the 3rd beat will be the **space** between numbers 3 and 4, and

the 4th beat will be the **space** between numbers 4 and 1.

Unlike Indian music western music does not have a **0 beat**, which is called **Khali**. Western music starts on the 1st beat.

The symbols which represent the sounds are called notes. They have sound values to them. When written on the staff, the note symbols represent the different lengths of sound, thus, making the rhythm of music. Rhythm may then be defined as the combination of all the long and short sounds in a piece of music within a specific beat. In other words the combination of all the different kinds of notes in a piece of music. There are basically four types of Rhythm from which all music is written. These are as follows:

1. A rhythm where the sound is more than one beat (single space of time) or in other words a note represents two or more beats of sound.

2. A rhythm where the sound is equal to one beat (single space of time) or a note represents one beat of sound.

3. A rhythm where the single beat (single space of time) will have two sounds which means that the beat is divided into two sounds which are equal in length.

4. A rhythm where the single beat (space of time) will have three or four or more sounds within the beat and these are also equally divided.

Western music is also divided into sections or divisions which we call Measures which are formed by vertical lines on the staff which we call Bar Lines. The beat in western music is grouped normally in double, triple, or quadruple time that is 2, 3 or 4 beats per measure. We find this in the time signature which is a set of two numbers one above the other. These numbers are normally found in the beginning of a piece of music.

Just as we speak in sentences to make sense in music we also have musical sentences which we call phrases and which normally consist of four measures of sound but which may also vary depending on the composition. These musical sentences are marked by curved lines called Slurs. These lines are found over a set of notes on the staff which indicate the phrase of music which expresses an idea. A complete sentence would normally consists of two phrases, the first called the **statement** and the second the **response**. These musical phrases or sentences usually end in a form of punctuation which we call **cadences** in music. They denote the end of a phrase.

All music is based on scales hence scales are the skeleton or backbone of any musical composition. In western music we have two basic kinds of scales - the Major scales and the Minor scales. The Minor scales are of three types - these are Natural minor, the Harmonic minor and the Melodic minor scales. Scales are built on a pattern of Tones and semitones. These tones and semitones are the distances of sounds. The semitones are the closest distance of two notes or pitches while the tones are two semitones side by side. Basing on the pattern of tones and semitones scales are identified as whether they are sharp scales or flat scales. A **sharp scale** is when the natural note of the scale is *raised* by a semitone and a **flat scale** is when the natural note of the scale is *lowered* by a semitone.

For example:
G majoi the notes are G A B C D E F$^\sharp$ G
F major the notes are F G A B$^\flat$ C D E F

All together we have about sixty scales in western music, these include all the majors and their relative minors, in all 3 forms. The *number of sharps or flats* in them we call the **key signature** of a scale. This includes the three types of minor scales as mentioned earlier. One may compare scales to multiplication tables in school which need to be learnt if we want to understand music properly. They are most essential in music learning.

Another very important aspect of western music is the skill of reading music which is most important if one is to be a good musician. For this we learn to identify **notes** on the staff, that is the lines and spaces, by the **distances** between them as they are **written on the staff,** up or down the staff. We call this Intervals between notes. We know that there are eight notes to a scale hence we number them as 1 2 3 4 5 6 7 8 or call them the eight degrees of a scale. Basing on this we identify the intervals between notes written on the lines and spaces. The following are the intervals identified.

1. Repeat - This is the interval of notes on the same line or space on the staff.

eg. Notes on the same second line or same third space.

2. Second - (Step) - The interval from a line note to a space note up or down.

eg. Notes on the 1st line and the 1st space up or notes on the 4th space and 4th line down.

3. Third - (Skip) - The interval from a line note to the next line note or from a space note to the next space note up or down.

eg. 3rd line note to 4th line note up or 2nd space note to 1st space note down.

4. Fourth - (3rd + 2nd) - The interval from a line note to a space note or space note to a line note up or down with a space and line in between.

eg. 1st line note to 2nd space note up or 4th line note to 2nd space note down.

5. Fifth - (3rd + 3rd) - The interval from a line note to a line note or space note to a space note up or down with a line or space in between.

eg. 1st line note to 3rd line note up or 3rd space note to 1st space note down.

Interval reading helps in getting the right pitch (sound) and the correct finger to play on the instrument. This skill of reading is most helpful for a smooth flowing production of sound on any instrument.

Points To Remember for Combined Notation System

Before using combined notation system the musicians should bear the following points in mind.

1. **The middle point C is fixed for every song, *Raga* or tune. The Sa or C note is compulsory. All tunes are based on the C note.**

2. **G note [P] cannot be changed into a half tone (flat) or a sharp note.**

3. **C and G cannot be omitted at a time in any *Raga*.**

The Symbol of matra on the staff notation is accepted by our combined notation system. It is equal to one *matra* time. Symbols of No. 1 and No. 2 are not used in combined notation system. The remaining fractional *matra* time symbols may be used as they are. The position of symbol of time notes in the clefs are accepted as they are.

Symbols of half tone notes (flats) and the sharp note are accepted. The symbol of extension of sound [—] is accepted for prolonging the notes, not for ending the sound. This symbol denotes one matra time. The symbol of prolonging notes for meend without dots are accepted as [ ] and for combined notes as [ ].

In the Indian Music system there are a number of taal variations which are not used in western music. Not only this, western music uses the taal with evenly spaced numbers only but in Indian music we have a number of taals which are odd and very complicated to play and understand. The notation of these taals and compositions set to these taals are naturally very hard to grasped.

There are a number of expressions such as 1.75 times of a beat, or .25 times of a beat, or 2.75 of a beat in Indian music notation system.

These expressions should be understood in Indian system only and be mastered in order to have a better command over the music of any form.

Part – 2
The Harmonium –
Then & Now

The Harmonium

The Harmonium is most widely known and used as a free-reed instrument of India. A free reed is a small strip of material made of metal. As a result, when pressure (or suction) is applied, the reed swings freely in a slot to set up a vibrating column of air which gives voice to the instrument. Be it in classical, light, film or folk music, the Harmonium makes its presence felt in every type of music played in India.

The Indian Harmonium is not a heavy and big pedal instrument but a small portable box. On its top is a keyboard like that of a piano, but with a much smaller range, usually of about three and half octaves. This is played by one hand, while the other works the bellows. It consists of a set of free reeds, whose length determines their pitch, activated by a wind supply from a hand-operated compression bellows controlled by a keyboard. The reed is responsible for the tone and pitch, whereas the air bellows produce and control the passing air and are responsible for the volume of the instrument. When the bellows are compressed, the air passes under the reed vibrating it, thus producing the desired pitch.

Today, the Harmonium maybe considered as a twin to any kind of Indian music. It is used almost in every type of music followed here. Some of the popular music forms such as: bhajans, ghazals or light music can not be imagined without the assistance of a Harmonium. With its unique sound and closeness with the human voice, the Harmonium is actually an important part of the entire music system.

History & Development

Christian Gottlieb Kratzenstein (1723-1795), Professor of Physiology at Copenhagen, was credited with the first free reed instrument to be made in the western world. With continuous changes and improvements made in the process, the harmonium, as we know it today, was invented in Paris in 1842 by Alexandre Debain.

The Harmonium reached the height of its popularity in the West in the late 19th and early 20th centuries. It generally weighs less than similar-sized pianos and is not easily damaged in transport. An added attraction to the Harmonium in tropical regions was that the instrument held its tune regardless of heat and humidity, unlike the piano. The 'export' market was sufficiently lucrative for manufacturers to produce harmoniums with cases impregnated with chemicals to prevent wood worm and other damaging organisms found in the tropics.

Although the harmonium was a popular instrument in the late-nineteenth century, changes in musical taste led to its decline early in the 1900's. The decline of interest, which began about 1930, was due to a change in musical taste. Music in the home as well as musical education in general turned increasingly away from the musical style of the 19th century. The harmonium and everything connected with it fell under the heading of 'kitsch.' Even in light music it was ousted by its more wieldy cousin, the accordion. Above all, however, with the advent of a whole range of electronic instruments, rival instruments have appeared which not only far surpass the sound combinations and expressive possibilities of the harmonium as a solo or accompanying instrument, but match completely the world of modern musical sounds. In sacred music, where the harmonium had taken the place of the organ, it has in its turn been replaced by either a small portable organ or an electronic organ. Just when the harmonium had reached its peak technically it became musically redundant and was laid aside."

At the peak of the instrument's popularity around 1900, a wide variety of styles of harmoniums were produced. These ranged from simple models with plain cases and only 4 or 5 stops (if any at all), up to large instruments with ornate cases, up to a dozen stops and other mechanisms such as couplers.

The invention of the electronic organ in the mid 1930s, spelt the end of the harmonium's success. It's popularity as a household instrument declined in the 1920s as musical tastes changed.

With so many in born qualities to match any form of music and able to be accommodated in many parts of the world, the Harmonium gradually travelled all over the world. In due course, it came to India where people took this sweet and portable instrument into their musical fraternity and made it an integral part of their music system. How the harmonium came to India and who brought it here is a debatable subject. But it is certain during the mid 19th century missionaries brought French-made hand-pumped Harmoniums to India. Its popularity has stayed intact to the present day and the Harmonium remains an important instrument in many genres of Indian music. It is commonly found in Indian homes. Though derived from the designs developed in France, the harmonium was developed further in India in unique ways, such as the addition of drone stops and a scale changing mechanism.

The Harmonium is essentially an alien instrument to the Indian tradition, as it cannot mimic the voice, which is considered the basis of all Indian music. *Meend* (glissando), an integral part of any classical recitation is not possible on the harmonium, and as such, one cannot reproduce the subtle nuances of a Raga on this instrument. The Harmonium is thus despised by many connoisseurs of Indian music, who prefer the more authentic yet more technical sarangi, in accompanying khyal singing.

Its popular usage is by followers of various Hindu and Sikh faiths, who use it in their devotional singing of prayers, called bhajan or kirtan. There will be at least one Harmonium in any Mandir (Hindu temple) or Gurdwara (Sikh temple) around the world. The Harmonium is also commonly accompanied by the tabla. To Sikhs the Harmonium is known as the vaja/baja. It is also referred to as a "Peti" (A loose reference to a "Box") in some parts of North India and Maharashtra.

It also forms an integral part of the Qawali repertoire, as many Qawwals use a Harmonium when performing Qawalis. It has received international fame as the genre of Qawali music has been popularized by renowned Pakistani musicians such as Nusrat Fateh Ali Khan and Aziz Mian.

In short, we may conclude with this that the Harmonium is inevitable and an inseparable part of music. It has great uses and it serves a lot when it comes to support and in aid of music.

Wind Instruments

Classical Indian Music mentions wind instruments as 'Sushir Vadya', the instruments that produces sound due to the pressure of air through them. The natural Instruments used in the ancient times are flutes of various types Shankh (sea shells) and the animal horns. Later on the reeds are introduced and the second type of wind instruments came into practice, where the wind is blown and indirectly it goes through the reed chamber to produce sounds of notes.

Various ancient wind Instruments are:

1. Flute
2. Shehnai
3. Nagaswaram
4. Sundari
5. Mukhveena
6. Narh
7. Algoza
8. Pavri
9. Pungi
10. Shankh
11. Thunchen
12. Khanglign
13. Mashak
14. Surnai
15. Bankia
16. Khung
17. Bans
18. Mohuri
19. Kol
20. Ransinga
21. Limbu

The second type of wind instruments are of reed Instrument. The main instrument in this category is the Harmonium. A very popular instrument of north India, consists of reeds and bellows to blow air inside. Other reed instruments of India are:

1. Harmonium

2. Nadaswaram (South India)

3. Mouth Organ

Wind Instruments, and how they look like:

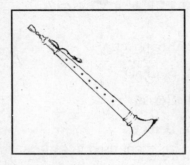

Shehnai

It is a popular wind instrument with holes on it to produce notes. It is used mostly in North Indian Music.

Nagaswaram

Popularly known as 'Mangal Vadya', it is used in Carnatic Music.

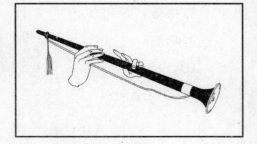

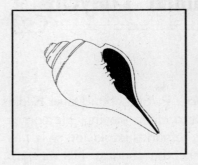

Shankh

Found in nature as a natural sea shell, it is widely used in homes during worship of Hindu Gods

Pungi

It is an instrument used by snake charmers. It is used in folk music also.

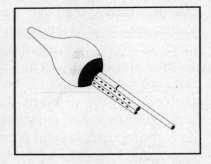

Mouth Organ

It is a popular reed instrument used in various types of music such as Jazz, Blue, Classical and many more

Out of these wind instruments, Bansuri is the most widely acceptable and used. It can be taken as the basic instrument for the development of modern day wind instruments.

Famous Harmonium Players

Pt. Shambhu Dayal Kedia : Pt Shambhu Dayal Kedia is a torch bearer in the field of Harmonium playing. He comes from a referred musical family. His remarkable playing style has earned him name and fame all over the country. His mastery over the Harmonium and playing it in *gayaki-ang* as well as instrumental style is the brand name of *Shambhuji*. He has the honor of playing solo Harmonium in so many musical concerts all over the country. The Harmonium literally sings in the accomplished hands of Pt. Shambhu Dayal Kedia. He has also performed with so many leading artists of the day as an accompanist on the Harmonium. A veteran musician and *guru*, he is continuously busy in promoting music and the Harmonium among music socities of the country. The field of Harmonium owes a lot to Shambhuji, since he has done a great deal in achieving status to the Harmonium what it has today in the field of music.

Shri Mahmud Dhoulpuri : The name of Mahmud Dhoulpuri has become synonymous with the Harmonium. He has attained distinct recognition in Harmonium playing as an accompanist artist. No concert is up to the mark without the inclusion of Shri *Dhoulpuriji*. For his enormous effort and continuous service to music, the government of India has conferred the prestigious *Padma Shree* award on Shri Dhoulpuriji. A well talked about name and a true gentleman, he is the man who has given a respectable place to Harmonium playing.

50

Part – 3
Know The
Harmonium

Types of Harmonium

The Harmonium we see today comes in so many forms and varieties depending upon the requirement and taste of the player. Harmonium making has technically become so advanced and complicated that today we have a number of varieties available in the market.

Starting from a single reed harmonium to the much advanced organ harmonium and scale changer available for music lovers. The harmoniums available now are suitable for different purposes, like for frequent travellers, there is a suitcase type harmonium, which is portable and safe to carry from one place to another. Similarly, harmoniums for playing ghazals and devotional accompaniments. There is an organ harmonium, which has a soft quality tone.

Most of the harmoniums are provided with drones. These are not very widely used but if we are playing pure classical music based on Indian *Ragas* then these drones come in handy. It gives a continues sound of the scale and prominent note of the raga as is provided by a tanpura.

Then there are harmoniums which have range of octaves to choose from and harmoniums with scale changers that allow different scales from the same group of keys.

The reeds now come in various types and shapes. Reeds of previous Harmoniums were made of wooden carvings now replaced by brass reeds, which are more durable and maintenance free.

Of course these varieties have a wide range of utility but financially there affordability is a major aspect. But as a beginner one should focus on a harmonium that is suitable for your basic need and at a reasonable price.

The major types of harmonium and their usage, available in the market, are given below:

1. **Simple Harmonium:** This type of harmonium is generally available to every music lover these days. It has 42 keys and one bellow. Three or three and half octaves can be played on this harmonium. This harmonium could be used in any form of music say vocal or instrumental. Beginners are taught basics of music on this particular harmonium. This harmonium does not resonate so profoundly because it has only one reed board. This harmonium is most suitable for beginners as it is reasonably priced and does not require too much maintenance.

2. **Coupler Harmonium:** It is almost like a simple harmonium but with an additional reed board. This additional reed board is situated between the upper reed board and the keys. The additional reed board is connected to the upper reed board and that is why when a note is played, the same note is sounded automatically from the additional reed board. This way two notes are sounded simultaneously. *Qawalli*, Bhajan *Mandali* or Play groups often use this type of harmonium. This is also known as the Double Reed Harmonium. This harmonium has more resonance as compared to the simple Harmonium.

3. **Suitcase or Folding type Harmonium:** This kind of harmonium looks like a suitcase. There is no basic difference in a coupler, simple or a suitcase type harmonium. It is different from other harmoniums in that it is cupped in a suitcase-like box. It can be carried very simply from one

place to another. Bellows of this kind of harmonium is fitted into the wooden cavity. When this Harmonium is opened it looks like any other Harmonium. Nomadic Play Groups often use this Harmonium for its convenience in transporting. It is more expensive than other Harmoniums due to its adaptive advantages. It also requires regular oiling to its hinges as one needs to open the box again and again in order to operate it

4. **Scale Changer Harmonium:** This is a Harmonium like the simple Harmonium. Its difference being that its keys are not attached to the keyboard but has a separate board. This separate board is attached to a thin sheet of leather. With the help of this leather sheet it is shifted forward or backward. When this sheet is brought forward or backward, the entire key board is shifted one note backward or forward thus allowing the player a different note from the same set of keys. This harmonium is useful for players who practice only on one set of keys.

5. **Organ Harmonium:** This type of Harmonium can be played by both hands and feet. The bellows are attached to the footrest of the Harmonium. It is operated with the help of the feet. The shape resembles that of a box. To decrease the size it can be folded inwards. The lower part of such Harmonium regulates the air flow and the upper part controls the keys. The main utility of this type of Harmonium is that the player is free to use both his hands on the finger board, thus allowing him to play chords or single notes accordingly. The player is also free to provide rhythm from the keys according to the beat of the tune. This type of Harmonium is generally used in plays or groups or professional concerts. The sound quality of this type of Harmonium is much louder as compared to other Harmoniums.

Difference of Harmonium on the Basis of Octaves

Harmoniums can also be classified on the basis of different octaves. There are Harmoniums available in the market with different octaves such as three octaves, three and quarter octaves or three and half octaves. Genaerally, quality-wise there is no difference in different octave Harmoniums. The only difference is that the Harmonium with more octaves can play a wider range of notes.

The human voice has a limitation in respect to the octaves that it can achieve. Normally the human voice can sing upto three octaves only. Here again there is some limitation. The Human voice cannot sing in the complete three octaves but some notes, either in lower or higher pitches, have to be ignored. In an instrument there is no such limitation.

A piano or an electronic organ has five or six or more octaves in it. The main advantage of these octaves is that they enrich the spectrum of the music. Notes and voices have different implication and effect in different octaves. A similar group of notes or a particular tune may have altogether different effect and ramifications in different octaves. It greatly depends upon the caliber and creativity of the musician to select the octave in which a tune has to be composed or played. In professional composition of music a greater range of octaves has a better advantage.

Thus the difference in harmoniums on the basis of octaves is mainly the availability of notes to be played. For a beginner, a harmonium with three octaves only will do the needful, but for a professional musician, a harmonium with a wider range of octaves is preferable.

The different octaves Harmonium are explained with the range of notes they can play on.

Harmonium on the basis of octaves

1. 3 Octave Harmonium

2. 3 ¼ octave Harmonium

3. 3 ½ octave Harmonium

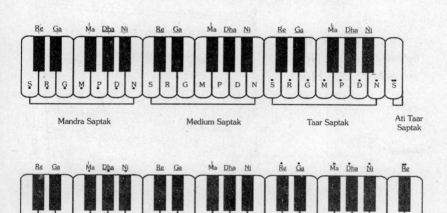

Parts of a Harmonium

Cover

Bellows

Key Springs

Keys

Stoppers

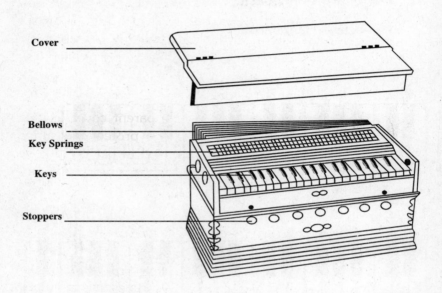

1. **Body or Box:** If you see the Harmonium, it looks like a box. That is how it is known in various parts of India, by the name of *peti,* which literally means the box. The body or the cover is actually a box made of seasoned wood that contains all the parts of a Harmonium. All the parts like the bellows, keys and reeds are fixed to the cover to produce the desired sounds. The cover of the Harmonium is made in different shapes and types according to various types of Harmoniums. There can be either just the box containing the playing Harmonium or the collapsible Harmonium fixed to the cover itself.

2. **Cover:** This is the common transparent cover fixed on top of the springs. The cover is to protect the springs from dust. The springs are protected to get the required sound for a longer time and to prevent the springs from rusting.

3. **Stoppers or Drones:** You can locate these stops in front of the Harmonium, below the keyboard. These lever-like stops when pulled are the air controllers of the reed board in the Harmonium. These stops and drones, five in number, are fixed at a proper distance under the keys. The stops control the flow of air into the reed chambers and drones are used to control the unnecessary pressure of air drawn on other reeds. Indian musicians can create sounds of the *Tanpura* using these stops and drones.

4. **Keyboard:** In front of the Harmonium you find the most prominently visible part of the Harmonium, the keyboard. The keyboard is as we see in other keyboard instruments like the Piano or Synthesizers which have black and white keys. The white keys are to play the tones and the black keys to play the semitones.

The total number of keys on a Harmonium depends on the type of the Harmonium. There are usually 3 types i.e. full

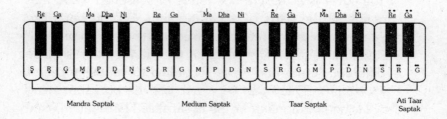

3 octaves has 37 keys, 3.1/4 octaves has 39 keys and 3.1/2 octaves has 42 keys.

The most common in practice is the one with 42 keys in which 24 keys are white and 18 keys are black. These keys make three and half octaves. Keys 1 to 12 make the higher octave, Keys 13 to 24 make the middle octave and Keys 25 to 36 make the lower octave. The remaining are of the double lower octave. Each octave has five black keys which are situated between a pair of white keys.

According to the western music system, the Harmonium is played as an accompanying instrument, so the Tonic or starting note can be on any white key and playing can be started with that key.

According to the India music system the tonic 'C' note is fixed. Harmonium here is played as a solo instrument, so the middle 'C' can be considered as any black key and playing can be started with any black key on the keyboard.

5. **Springs:** These are brass springs attached behind the keys. The main function of these springs are to pull the keys back to their original position, after they are played to produce sound.

6. **Reed Board:** This is the most important part of any wind instrument and certainly harmonium's too. This part is not visible from outside the harmonium, but plays a vital role in sound production.

   The reed board is a brass plate that has many holes. This board is fixed under the keyboard with keys on one side and holes on the other. On this reed board many reed plates which have several openings for air to pass are fixed. When the air passes through the air chamber of this reedboard, it produces vibrations and hence converts them into sounds. When pressing the keys the sounds are converted to notes.

7. **Bellows:** Another vital part of sound production in a Harmonium is the bellows. The bellows are the source of air pressure for the harmonium's reeds. The bellows are pumped by hand sucking air from outside and sending it into the reed board. The speed and volume of air sucked into the reeds depends on the type of the bellows.

   These bellows have one to five layers. The higher the number of layers the less effort on the left hand to produce the sound. In other words, the number of layers of bellows and effort of the left hand are inversely proportional. Not only this, the greater number of layers help produce the notes more easily and helps sustain the tone of the harmonium for a longer duration thus producing the effect of a 'Tanpura'. The bellows are made of cloth or plastic, which is pasted on to the wooden frame. Harmoniums with different bellows are dealt in detail below.

   Single Bellow: It has only one bellow glued to the outer wall on one side of the box and to the bellow board on the other side.

Single bellow

Double Bellow: It has two bellows attached at the place of one bellow.

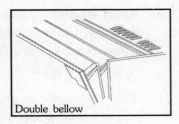

Double bellow

Triple Bellow : The bellows here has two joints connecting triple bellows.

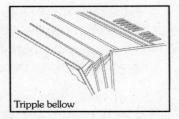

Tripple bellow

Five bellows: Here are five bellows attached to each other instead of one. These kinds of harmoniums are used by professionals.

Seven or Multifold Bellows: This has seven bellows attached together and have multifolds to chamber. These are also used by professional players.

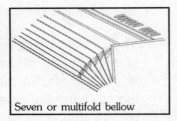

Seven or multifold bellow

The greater number of bellows are useful to suck in more air which helps in sustaining the notes for a longer duration. The players also can play longer with less air blowing.

8. Instruction manual or the reference book

This is another part or an accessory that should come along with the instrument you purchase. This provides the know how and maintenances tips for the instrument. It also guides you the basic introduction and playing technique for the Harmonium.

Part – 4
Playing The
Harmonium

Different Types of Sitting

Harmonium in India is played sitting on the floor, unlike the western style organ that is played by sitting on a stool or bench at a comfortable height. Different sitting styles are prevalent in India and one should choose accordingly.

Sitting Cross Legged

Before learning to play the Harmonium let us understand the ideal posture of sitting on the floor as practiced in India. Here the player sits on the floor keeping the feet crossed one over the other with the right knee over the left foot. This  popular posture is somehow easy and does not produce pain even when sitting for a long time. We can place the notebook over and adjacent to the keyboard for quick glances at it when needed.

1. When you are comfortably seated, now place the harmonium in front of you keeping the right hand over the keyboard and the left hand stretched over the bellows. This helps a player to practice for a longer period. It is the most common posture practiced in India. Often learners use this

65

sitting posture comfortable and easy as it allows a slight movement to the feet when one finds it a little inconvenience when sitting for a longer time initially.

2. Sitting on the floor. Now take the harmonium and place one side of it over the left thigh, leaving the other corner of the harmonium on the floor. This way the left hand is slightly raised and placed in a more convenient position to pump the bellows. The right hand will be closer to the body, which reduces  tension on the hand. This is called the *Qawwali* posture because it is often used by qawwali artists. This posture is specially suited for fast movements of the right hand over the keyboard. It is often used by folk artists of India when playing at communal gatherings and village celebrations.

3. This is the posture used by Westerners or by those who perform on stage in a concert. This posture is also getting popular these days because most *ghazal* singers and performing artists use Harmonium as their accompanying instrument. This posture allows a formal *eye* contact with the audience, so one can make facial expressions while singing.

☞ *If a player finds any difficulty in sitting according to the positions suggested above, he can keep the harmonium sideways and play it. Most westners find it difficult to sit on the ground, hence sit on a chair initially.*

Bellowing the Harmonium

The Bellows, as explained, are the most important part of the harmonium. The bellows identify the harmonium as a reed instrument from the piano, a keyboard instrument. The Bellows work to pump air into the reeds through air chambers made for this purpose. They also suck the air required in playing, to provide the pressure for sound creation by the harmonium.

Bellowing is a technique that needs to be understood and practiced well before learning to play the Harmonium. This is done by holding the bellow board at the end of the bellows using four fingers of the left hand and keeping a firm grip using the thumb at the edge of the bellows, which is on the harmonium box. When the bellow stretches to suck in air, the palm opens and when it closes, to fill the air into the reed chamber, the palm closes.

This practice of opening and closing the palm holding the two ends of the bellows makes bellowing possible in the Harmonium.

One should keep these points in mind when bellowing:

1. Too much bellowing is not required as it can tear the air-chamber and the joint of multifold bellows.

2. One must not bellow the harmonium without pressing the keys as it can distort the sound.

3. The pressure of the bellows should be just right, otherwise the notes would be too loud and unpleasant.

4. One must avoid pressing air into the air-chamber without opening a couple of stoppers as it can increase the pressure of air in the chamber which could lead to reed damage.

5. When playing is finished suck out all the air from the harmomium by pressing the keys after closing the bellows.

Fingers on the Harmonium

Only three fingers, that is Finger - 1, the index finger; Finger -2, the middle finger; and finger -3, the ring finger; are prominently used when playing the harmonium. The fourth finger and the thumb is rarely used, usually only on chords. These fingers must run in a disciplined sequence and should not jump or cross each other. The flow of the fingers should be like a stream, there should not be any stumble. Playing in a proper sequence of fingers gives a very artistic impression and nice to look at.

One should keep in mind the following points while using fingers on the keyboard:

Point 1. The hand and fingers should not be flat on the fingerboard. Rather the hand must be cup-shaped and fingers spread by the finger tips over the keys. This will allow the fingers to run smoothly without any disruption.

Point 2. The fingers must avoid crossing each other otherwise the desired notes could be missed.

Point 3. The first three fingers are mostly used, so a player should practice on these fingers only when playing or practicing.

Point 4. The pressure of the fingers on the keys need to be just right to get a sweet sound production.

Point 5. The thumb is usually played on white keys, but can be used when playing on the first black as middle 'C'.

Tips for Playing Harmonium

TIP 1 Be comfortable in the sitting posture of your choice.

TIP 2 Both hands should be relaxed but firm at their respective positions. Left hand on the bellows and right hand on the keyboard.

TIP 3 Start playing the bellows by keeping four fingers in front of the bellow board and thumb on the harmonium box. This will stretch the palm open as the bellows are open. Now pump the bellows by closing the palm reaching a constant speed of opening and closing the palm movement, pumping the bellows.

TIP 4 Use the stoppers and drones as required by the music to be played.

TIP 5 When playing the keys the tip of the fingers must only press the keys. Unnecessary touch of the palm or the hand can distort the sound or play undesired notes.

TIP 6 The speed of the bellow pumping must not change while playing. It must remain constant and at a regular pace.

TIP 7 Maintain a perfect coordination between the two-hand movements. The change in the movement of either of the hands can cause problems in playing. This will create a break in the rhythm.

69

TIP 8   The hands and the elbows must be parallel to the keyboard to prevent tiredness for the player.

TIP 9   The fingers and palm should be cup-shaped as the power to play must come from the hand rather than from the fingers. This will reduce the tension on the fingers.

TIP 10   The pressure on the keys should not exceed as to produce a hammering sound on the keyboard. It should be gentle enough for a smooth sound production.

TIP 11   Avoid crossing fingers while playing. The notes and fingers should be played in the ascending or descending order on the fingerboard according to the discipline of Harmonium playing and finger placement.

TIP 12   Sit up back straight at all times. A bad posture does not look good and is bad healthwise.

TIP 13   In Indian tradition, showing of feet while playing is not considered courteous, so try to keep the feet either covered by a cloth or hidden behind the Harmonium.

TIP 14   Avoid making unnecessary facial expressions. This is a sign of strain or stress and uneasiness. Try to be as natural as possible.

TIP 15   Unnecessary waving of hands or shaking the body is not considered a good playing gesture.

Part - 5
Notes on Harmonium

Playing Natural Notes on Harmonium

ॐ ════════════════════════════════ ॐ

We know that the Indian music system has seven natural notes, namely Sa, Re, Ga, Ma, Pa, Dha and Ni. When we add the sa of the next octave to these notes, it gives us a complete octave of eight notes. Again there are three octaves -

1. Middle octave (*Madhaya Saptak*)

2. Lower octave (*Mandra* saptak)

3. Upper or Higher octave (Tar Saptak)

Although we can play many octaves such as double lower and double higher as available in instruments like the piano, the basic octaves recognized are these three octaves that a human voice can reach.

The Harmonium is popular among the Indian music fraternity because it has unique playing arrangements. Unlike other wind and string instruments, we can play as many notes as our fingers can touch. The concept of chords, which is a basis of western music but not popular in Indian music is available on the Harmonium. When played with chords instead of playing single note it gives a captivating musical atmosphere. Sometimes a chord can express the very musical feelings that a single note cannot. Not only this, but rhythm could also be produced on the harmonium with a chord by moving the fingers according to the beat.

Here we will learn the production of basic natural notes on the Harmonium. It is possible to play two, three or more notes at a time. But for consistency start playing the notes one after another and practice their variations properly. After you reach a comfortable playing stage, then start playing groups of notes like the chords.

73

Playing the Natural Notes

Natural notes are the basic notes of music. It is the natural notes that is the basis to the flat or sharp notes. Whatever may be the scale of our playing, the flat or sharp notes will depend on the frequency difference of the natural notes. Thus in simple words the natural notes are the origins of all other notes of the theory of music.

In this book we have explained the notes from the middle octave which is more commonly used in singing and playing.

Playing the Natural Notes on the Middle Octave:

Note **Sa**: Sa is the most important note of any octave. It is the note that decides the other notes of the octave. It is fixed and does not have any flat or sharp. Sa note is played by pressing the first finger on the first black key which is numbered 14 on the fingerboard.

Note **Re**: It is the second note of any octave. This note also has a flat. But since we are playing the natural note only we have to press the second black key, numbered 16 on the finger board.

Note **Ga**: It is the third note of the octave. This note has a flat. To produce the natural note Ga, press the white key number 18 on the fingerboard. This will give 'Ga' note of the natural scale.

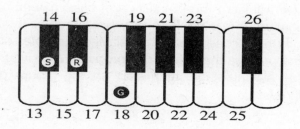

Note **Ma**: It is the fourth note of the octave. This is the only note which has a sharp only and not a flat. To produce the natural note of Ma on the finger board, press the black key number 19.

Note **Pa**: It is the fifth note of the octave. Like 'Sa' this is also a fixed note which does not have any flat or sharp. Natural note 'Pa' is produced by pressing the black key number 21 on the fingerboard.

Note **Dha**: It is the sixth note of the octave. It has a flat. To produce the natural note Dha, press the black key number 23 on the fingerboard.

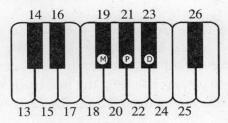

Note **Ni**: It is the seventh note of the octave. It also has a flat. To produce the natural Ni, press the white key number 25 on the fingerboard.

Note **'Sa'** of the higher octave: It is the same note as previous 'Sa' but differing in pitch only. It is produced by pressing the black key number 26 on the fingerboard from where the next octave starts.

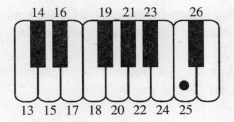

Flat & Sharp Notes

Flat and Sharp Notes are used both the Indian as well as the Western music system. These are micro tonal variations of the natural notes which are distinguishable from the other frequencies of sound. These flat and sharp notes not only add beauty to music but gives completeness to the human voice or instrumental music. Combined with the natural notes these flat and sharp notes make a complete range of voice or tone that enriches the music system.

Komal Re note: To produce the Flat Re on the finger board play the white key number 15 on the fingerboard. Remember, every other note is determined according to the note of Sa. Here we are following the first black key as Sa. So, pressing the white key number 15 on the fingerboard will give flat Re.

Komal Ga note: To produce flat Ga note play the white key number 17 on the fingerboard.

Teevra Ma note: It is the only note which is a sharp. To produce Teevra Ma play the white key number 20 on the finger board.

Komal Dha note: To produce the flat note of Dha, play the white key number 22 on the fingerboard.

Komal Ni note: Flat note Ni is produced by playing the white key number 24 on the fingerboard.

Playing Tonic(1st Key)on White Keys

Harmonium playing can be started by taking any white key as the tonic (*Shuddha Sa*). We can play the tonic (First key of a scale) on any white key and start playing the complete octave from there on, however the place for the note 'C' is fixed on the Harmonium.

All the full tone natural notes are in sequence after Tonic note and all the flat notes and sharp notes are then played on either black or white keys depending on the starting tonic (1st) key position. The position of notes are explained below.

White keys	Notes (middle octave)	Black keys	Notes
13	Sa (*Shuddha*)	14	Re (Komal)
15	Re	16	Ga (Komal)
17	Ga	19	Ma (Komal)
18	Ma	21	Dha (Komal)
20	Pa	23	Ni (Komal)
22	Dha		
24	Ni		
25	Sa (*upper octave*)		

Practice the complete octave according to the chart and the picture of the keyboard given below.

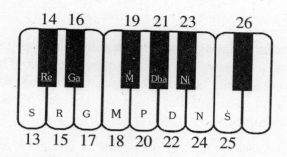

(Medium Octave Exercise)

*Remember this type of method is used in western music system.

Playing Tonic (1st key) on Black Keys

Harmonium playing can also be started by taking any black key as the Tonic (*Shuddha Sa*). We can play the tonic (1st key) on any black key and derive the complete octave from there on. The position of middle 'C' however, is fixed on the keyboard.

All the full tone natural notes are in sequence after the tonic note and all the flat notes and sharp notes are then derived on either black or white keys depending on the starting tonic key position. The position of notes according to a black key as the first playing key are explained below.

Black keys	Notes (middle octave)	White keys	Notes
14	Sa (Shuddha)	15	Re (Komal)
16	Re	17	Ga (Komal)
18	Ga (Shuddha)		
19	Ma	20	Ma (Tivra)
21	Pa	22	Dha (Komal)
23	Dha	24	Ni (komal)
		25	Ni (Shuddha)
26	Sa (upper octave)		

Practice the complete octave as according to the chart and the picture of the keyboard given below.

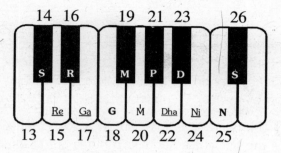

(Medium Octave Exercise)

* Remember this type of method is used in Indian music system, where Harmonium is played along with singing.

Songs on Harmonium

Song: Main Koi aisa geet gaaon

Film name : Yess Boss
Music by:Jatin Lalit

Singer : Abhijeet
Lyrics by Javed Akhtar

Beat : Kahrava

1	2	3	4	5	6	7	8	1	2	3	4	5	6	7	8
–	–	–	–	–	–	–	–	–	–	–	–	s	main	ko	i
–	–	R	–	–	–	R	–	–	–	R	–	–	P	D	P
ai	sa	gee	t	gaa	s	oon	s	s	s	s	s	s	s	s	ke
N	N	N	P	D	–	D	–	–	–	–	–	–	–	–	–
aa	r	zoo	ja	gaa	s	oon	a	s	s	s	s	s	s	s	s
N	N	N	P	D	–	D	–	–	–	–	–	–	P	D	P
gar	s	s	s	tum	s	s	ka	ho	s	s	s	s	s	s	s
G	–	–	–	Ṁ	–	–	Ṁ	P	–	–	–	NṠ	RĠ	MP	D
–	–	–	–	–	–	–	–	–	–	–	–	s	main	ko	i
G	–	–	–	Ṁ	–	–	Ṁ	P	–	–	–	–	P	D	P
ai	sa	gee	t	gaa	s	oon	ke	aa	r	zoo	ja	gaa	s	oon	a
N	N	N	P	D	–	D	P	N	N	N	P	D	–	D	P
gar	s	s	s	tum	s	s	ka	ho	s	s	s	s	s	s	s
G	–	–	–	Ṁ	–	–	Ṁ	P	–	–	–	–	–	–	–
tum	s	ko	bu	laa	s	oon	yeh	pal	s	ke	bi	chhaa	s	oon	ka
Ṙ	–	Ṙ	N	Ś	–	N	Ṙ	Ṙ	–	Ṙ	N	Ś	–	N	Ṙ
dam	s	tum	ja	han	ja	han	ra	kho	s	s	s	s	za	mee	ko
R	–	Ġ	Ś	Ṙ	Ś	Ṙ	S	D	–	–	–	–	P	D	PM
aa	s	maan	ba	naa	s	oon	si	taa	ron	se	sa	jaa	s	oon	a
N	N	N	P	D	–	D	P	N	N	N	P	D	–	D	PM

1	2	3	4	5	6	7	8	1	2	3	4	5	6	7	8
gar	s	s	s	tum	s	s	ka	ho	s	s	s	s	main	ko	i
G	–	–	–	Ṁ	–	–	Ṁ	P	–	–	–	–	P	D	P
ai	sa	gee	t	gaa	s	oon	ke	aa	r	zoo	ja	gaa	s	oon	a
N	N	N	P	D	–	D	P	N	N	N	P	D	–	D	–
gar	s	s	s	tum	s	s	ka	ho	s	s	s	s	s	s	s
G	–	–	–	Ṁ	–	–	D	N	–	–	P	–	–	–	–
–	–	–	–	–	–	–	–	s	main	tit	li	yon	ke	pee	chhe
Ṡ	N	D	P	M	G	R	S	N	Ṙ	N	Ṡ	Ṙ	Ġ	Ṁ	Ġ
bhaa	s	goon	s	s	s	s	s	s	main	jug	nu	on	ke	pee	chhe
Ṙ	Ġ	Ṙ	–	–	–	–	–	–	Ġ	Ṙ	Ġ	Ṙ	Ġ	Ṙ	Ġ
jaa	s	oon	s	s	s	s	s	s	yeh	ran	g	hai	voh	ro	sh
Ṡ	–	D	D	N	D	N	D	P	Ṙ	N	Ṡ	Ṙ	Ġ	Ṁ	Ġ
ni	s	hai	s	s	s	s	s	s	tum	haa	re	paa	s	do	no
Ṙ	Ġ	Ṙ	–	–	–	–	–	–	Ġ	Ṙ	Ġ	Ṙ	Ġ	Ṙ	Ġ
laa	s	oon	s	s	s	s	s	jit	ni	khush	bu	ein	s	s	s
Ṡ	–	D	–	–	–	–	–	Ṡ	Ṡ	Ṡ	N	D	–	–	–
s	s	s	ss	ss	ss	s	s	baa	g	mein	mi	le	s	ss	s
Ṗ	–	Ṙ	ṘN	ḊP	ṀG	–	–	Ṙ	Ṙ	Ṙ	N	D	–	ḊN	Ṙ
s	s	s	s	s	s	Haan	s	jit	ni	khush	bu	ein	s	s	s
–	–	–	–	–	–	Ṡ	–	Ṡ	Ṡ	Ṡ	N	D	–	–	Ṙ
baa	g	mein	mi	le	s	s	Main	laa	oon	s	va	han	pe	s	ke
Ṙ	Ṙ	Ṙ	N	D	–	–	Ṁ	Ṁ	D	–	D	D	N	–	Ṡ
tum	s	ho	ja	han	ja	han	pe	e	k	pal	bhi	Theh	roon	s	main
Ṙ	–	Ṡ	Ṡ	N	P	D	P	N	–	N	P	D	D	–	P

1	2	3	4	5	6	7	8	1	2	3	4	5	6	7	8
gul	si	ta	ba	naa	oon	s	a	gar	s	s	s	tum	s	s	ka
N	N	N	P	D	D	–	P	G	–	–	–	M	–	–	M
ho	s	s	s	s	main	koi	s	–	–	–	–	–	–	–	–
P	–	–	–	–	–	–	–	–	–	–	–	–	–	–	–

Para II

Agar kaho to main suna-oon, tumhe hasi kahaniya

sunogi kya meri zubani, tum ek pari ki dastaan

ya main karoo tumse bayaan,

ho.. ya main karoo tum se bayaa,

ke raja ko rani mili thi kahan, kahaniyo ke nagar me

tumhe le ke jaa-oon, agar tum kaho,

tumko bula-oon ke palke bicha-oon,

kadam tum jaha-jaha rakho,

zami ko asma bana-oon, sitaro se saja-oon,

agar tum kaho....

main koi aisa geet gaa-oon........

(Other paras will be played as para I)

Song: Kal ho na ho

Film name : kal ho na ho
Music by Shankar,ehsan & loy
Singer : Sonu nigam
Lyrics by Javed Akhtar
Beat : Kahrava

1	2	3	4	5	6	7	8	1	2	3	4	5	6	7	8
–	–	–	–	–	–	–	–	–	–	–	–	–	–	–	–
Ṙ	–	–	–	Ġ	–	–	–	P	PṠ	PṠ	GP	P	PṠ	PṠ	GP

s	ss	ss	ss	s	ss	ss	ss	har	gha	di	ba	dal	ra	hi	hai
P	PṠ	PṠ	GP	P	PṠ	PṠ	GP	Ṡ	N	Ṡ	N	Ṡ	N	ṠĠ	Ṙ

roo	p	zi	nda	gi	s	s	s	chha	av	hai	ka	bhi	ka	bhi	hai
N	D	N	D	N	–	–	–	Ṡ	N	Ṡ	N	Ṡ	N	ṠĠ	Ṙ

dhoo	p	zi	nda	gi	har	pal	ya	han	s	s	s	s	jee	bhar	ji
N	D	N	D	N	P	D	Ṡ	D	–	–	–	–	M	P	D

yo	s	s	s	s	jo	hai	sa	ma	s	s	s	s	kal	ho	naa
P	–	–	–	–	P	D	Ṡ	D	–	–	–	PM	M	N̲	D

ho	s	s	s	s	s	s	s	(REPEAT)							
P	–	–	–	–	–	–	–								

PARA 1

s	ss	s	s	s	ss	s	s	s	chaa	he	jo	tu	mhe	s	poo	re
Ṙ	PṠ	–	–	D	NṠ	Ṡ	–	DP	N	Ṡ	MĠ	Ṙ	–	N	D

dil	s	se	s	s	s	s	s	s	mil	ta	hai	woh	s	mu	sh
N	–	Ṡ	–	Ṙ	–	D	–	–	N̲Ṡ	M	G	Ṙ	–	N	D

kil	s	se	s	s	s	ss	s	ss	ai	sa	jo	ko	s	i	ka
N	–	Ṡ	D	P	–	DP	D	N̲R	N̲Ṡ	M	Ġ	Ṙ	–	N	D

hin	s	hai	s	s	s	s	s	s	bas	vo	hi	sab	s	se	ha
N	–	Ṡ	–	D	–	Ṙ	–	Ṡ	N̲Ṡ	M	Ġ	ṘṘ	–	N	D

86

1	2	3	4	5	6	7	8	1	2	3	4	5	6	7	8
seen	s	hai	s	s	us	haa	th	ko	s	s	ss	s	tum	thaa	m
N	–	Ṡ	D	P	P	D	Ṡ	D	–	–	ND	M	M	P	D
lo	s	s	ss	s	vo	mehe	r	ba	s	s	s	s	kal	ho	na
P	–	–	SG	R	P	D	Ṡ	D	–	–	P	M	M	N	D
ho	s	s	s	s	har	pal	ya	ha	s	s	s	s	ji	bhar	ji
P	–	–	SG	R	P	D	Ṡ	D	–	–	P	M	M	N	D
yo	s	s	s	s	jo	hai	sa	ma	s	s	s	s	kal	s	ho
P	–	–	–	–	P	D	Ṡ	ṠR	D	–	P	M	M	–	N
s	na	ho	s	s	s	s	s	s	s	s	s	s	s	s	s
–	D	P	–	–	–	–	–	–	–	–	–	–	–	–	–

Para II

palko ke le ke saaye aansu koi jo aaye

lakh sambhalo pagal dil ko dil dhadke hi jaaye

par soch lo is pal hai jo, vo dastan kal ho na ho

har ghadi ....

Song: Pehla Nasha Pehla Khumaar

Film name : Jo jeeta wohi Sikandar   Singer : Udit Nrn, Sadhna
Music by:Jatin Lalit   Lyrics by Majrooh sult.

Beat : Kahrava

&ℰ ══════════════════════════════════ ℭℬ

1	2	3	4	5	6	7	8	1	2	3	4	5	6	7	8
–	chaahe	tum	kuch	na	ka	ho	s	s	maine	sun	li	ya	s	s	s
Ṁ	DP	P	M	M	P	K	–	–	DN	DP	M	M	–	–	–
s	Ke	saa	thi	pyaa	r	Ka	s	s	mujhe	chun	li	ya	s	chun	li
–	D	DP	M	Ṡ	Ṡ	P	–	–	DN	DP	M	M	–	MP	D
ya	s	s	s	s	maine	sun	li	ya	s	s	s	s	s	s	s
P	–	–	–	–	PD	MP	D	P	–	–	–	–	–	–	–
s	Peh	la	na	sha	s	s	Peh	la	Khu	maa	r	s	s	s	s
Ṁ	DD	Ṡ	Ṡ	ṠṘ	Ṡ	–	PM	P	Ṡ	Ṡ	–	–	–	–	–
s	naya	pyaa	r	hai	s	s	naya	in	tezaa	s	r	s	s	s	kar
M	DD	Ṡ	Ṡ	ṠṘ	Ṡ	–	ND	P	PP	D	P	–	–	–	MG
loon	mainky	ap	na	haa	l	s	s	Ae	dile	be	qa	raa	s	r	me
R	GM	D	P	P	–	–	–	R	GM	D	P	P	–	–	MG
re	dile	be	qa	raa	r	tu	hiba	ta	s	s	s	s	s	s	s
R	GM	D	P	P	P	MP	DM	P	–	–	–	–	–	–	–
s	Peh	la	na	sha	s	s	Peh	la	Khu	maa	s	s	s	s	r
–	DD	Ṡ	Ṡ	Ṙ	–	–	P	D	Ṙ	ṠṘ	Ṡ	–	–	–	–
s	sss	s	s	s	s	s	s	ud	taa	s	hi	phiru	s	s	inha
M	MPM	–	–	N	–	D	–	Ṁ	Ṁ	Ṡ	Ṙ	GR	–	–	ṘṠ

1	2	3	4	5	6	7	8	1	2	3	4	5	6	7	8
waa	on	s	mein	Kahin	s	ss	s	ya	main	jhoo	l	jaa	oon	s	ingha
N	P	–	Ṙ	Ṡ̱Ṡ	Ṡ	Ṡ̱Ṙ	Ṡ	M̱G	M	Ṙ	G̱	M	Ṙ	–	Ṛ̱Ṡ
Taa	on	s	mein	kahin	s	s	ss	s	s	ss	ss	s	s	s	s
N	P	–	Ṙ	Ṡ̱Ṡ	–	–	Ṡ̱Ṙ	G̱	Ṙ	G̱M	G̱Ṙ	Ṡ	Ṁ	–	–
ud	ta	s	hi	phiru	s	s	inha	wao	on	s	mein	Kahin	s	s	s
Ṁ	Ṁ	Ṡ	Ṙ	G̱Ṙ	–	–	Ṛ̱Ṡ	–	N	P	Ṙ	Ṡ̱Ṡ	–	–	–
ya	main	jhoo	l	jaa	oon	s	ingha	Taa	on	s	mein	Kahin	s	s	ek
M̱G	M	Ṙ	G̱	Ṁ	Ṙ	–	Ṛ̱Ṡ	N	P	–	Ṙ	Ṡ̱Ṡ	–	–	Ṡ̱N
Kar	doon	aa	s	maan	s	s	aur	zami	s	s	s	s	s	s	Kaho
Ṡ	Ṙ	G̱	Ṙ	Ṡ	–	–	Ṡ	ṈṠ	–	–	–	–	–	–	Ṡ̱N
yaa	ron	kya	ka	hoon	s	s	Kya	nahin	s	s	s	s	s	s	s
Ṡ	Ṙ	G̱	Ṁ	Ṉ	–	–	ṈṠ	ḎN	–	–	–	–	–	–	–
s	peh	la	na	sha	s	s	s	s	s	s	ss	ss	ss	s	s

Para II

Usne baat ki kuch aise Dhang se

Sapne de gaya wo hazaro rang ke

rah jaa-oon jaise main haar ke

aur choome wo mujhe pyaar se

pehla nasha...............

Notes

Notes

Notes

PANKAJ PUBLICATIONS

≡ Suggested Readings on Keyboard Instruments ≡

Learn to Play on Harmonium

ISBN: 81-87155-22-1

A Bestseller book of the popular 'Learn to Play series', talks about learning the worlds' favourite instrument in detail. Pictorial details of handling, postures and tuning the instrument for the comfort of every learner. A sure pick for the learners.

Harmonium - Learn & Play

Hindi - ISBN: 81-87155-88-4

A Detail book on Harmonium Learning with color pictures explaining positions, postures and playing. The book is available in both HINDI & ENGLISH language. Comes along with an audio C.D. Explains sounds of the Harmonium.

PANKAJ PUBLICATIONS

- Presents -

Practice books for music Learners

SELECTED HINDI SONGS
WITH NOTATIONS & CHORDS

The series presents the songbooks in the form of collection of songs for early musicians to practice. The notations with the songs let learners practice to play the songs on Indian Notation System and on chords. The series has collection of songs in Hindi, as well as their romanized version for easy readability for English speaking people.

PANKAJ PUBLICATIONS

Learn to Play on... Series

For Information or to Order,

Please visit our website: **www.pankajmusic.com**
or Email us at: contact@pankajmusic.com
or simply write to: **Pankaj Publications, 3, Regal Building, Sansad Marg, New Delhi - 1100 01.**